Mummies
Don't Coach
Softball

There are more books about the Bailey School Kids!
Have you read these adventures?

Mummies Don't Coach Softball

by **Debbie Dadey**
and
Marcia Thornton Jones

illustrated by **John Steven Gurney**

A
LITTLE APPLE
PAPERBACK

SCHOLASTIC INC.
New York   Toronto   London   Auckland   Sydney

ISBN 0-590-22639-8

12 11   8 9/9 0 1/0

Printed in the U.S.A.
First Scholastic printing, May 1996

Book design by Laurie Williams

*For Thelma Thornton and Rebecca Bailey Gibson
and for all good "mummies" everywhere
— MTJ and DD*

Contents

1

Coach Tuttle

Eddie spit in his hat before slapping it over his curly red hair.

"Why did you do that?" Howie asked.

"For good luck," Eddie said. "And we need all the luck we can get to beat the Sheldon Slammers today!"

"Aw, we'll whip their sorry team," Melody said.

"But no Bailey team has ever won at Antwerp Field," Howie reminded them.

"Well, just to be sure, I hope you all wore your lucky underwear!" Eddie told them.

Melody giggled. "I hope you wore clean underwear. That would make us all lucky!"

Eddie, Howie, Melody, and Liza headed to the Antwerp softball field. Today was the fifth game of the season. So far they had won every game, but this was their first game at Antwerp Field.

Howie swung his bat through the air. "Coach Ellison is the best coach the Bailey Batters ever had. I bet we win the third grade championship this year."

Liza skipped along beside her friends. "You're right. We're lucky to have Coach Ellison. He's a good coach!"

"But you don't like softball," Melody told her friend.

"I do now!" Liza said. "Coach Ellison showed me how much fun it can be!"

The four friends rushed to join the rest of their team across the field. The Sheldon Slammers were huddled around their coach. A few of them stuck out their tongues when Eddie, Melody, Howie, and Liza jogged by. Melody had to grab Eddie's arm to keep him from causing trouble.

The rest of the Bailey Batters stood

near the bleachers. A fat player named Huey was blowing huge pink bubbles and Carey was having a pushing contest with Sam. Nobody looked ready to play.

"Where's Coach Ellison?" Liza asked Carey.

Carey flipped her blonde curls away from her face and shrugged. "Nobody's seen him since last week."

Huey plucked the pieces of a popped bubble from his chin. "My mom heard Coach Ellison won a cruise. I bet he's soaking up sun rays in the Bahamas right now."

"But he can't!" Melody squealed. "He has to help us win our game against the Sheldon Slammers!"

The entire team glanced across the field. The Sheldon Slammers glared back. Liza stepped behind Howie and frowned. "What are we going to do? They look like they ate softballs for breakfast."

"Liza's right," Eddie said. "We don't

have a jelly bean's chance of winning without Coach Ellison."

"Perhaps I can help," a strange voice interrupted.

The Bailey Batters turned around to face the stranger. His jet-black hair was cut in a straight line over his eyebrows. A bandage was stuck over his suntanned nose, but that wasn't his only bandage. He had two criss-crossed on his right hand and a bandage wrapped around his chin.

"I am Coach Tuttle," he told the team, his words clipped short by a foreign accent. "I was a coach once, a very long time ago. Coach Ellison asked me to help."

"What happened to you?" Eddie blurted.

"Eddie!" Liza hissed. "Be polite!"

Liza smiled sweetly. "We're the Bailey Batters. Welcome to our team. We can use all the help we can get."

Coach Tuttle smiled. "Then let us begin!" But when Coach Tuttle stepped off the bleachers, his foot got caught and he tumbled down, landing in a heap at the feet of the Bailey Batters.

"Oh, no!" Liza squealed. "He's not moving!"

2

Oops!

"Stand back," Eddie warned before stepping closer to the fallen coach. With the end of his softball bat, Eddie poked Coach Tuttle.

"Poke harder," Howie suggested.

But Eddie didn't have to, because the new coach started moaning. He sat up, shook his head, and smiled at the Bailey Batters. "I must have taken a little spill," he said.

Liza held out her hand to help up the coach. "We were worried. We thought you were dead."

Coach Tuttle grabbed her hand and tried to stand. "I'm okay," he said. "I believe just my ankle is twisted."

"Should we call a doctor?" Howie asked.

"No need," the strange coach said cheerfully. "I am quite experienced at wrapping limbs." Coach Tuttle reached for a black leather bag. He flipped open the rusty latch and dug inside.

"This will do the trick," he said and pulled out a big ball of white elastic bandage. Before anyone could offer to help, Coach Tuttle wound the bandage around and around until his ankle and half of his leg disappeared. When he was finished, he stepped carefully on his foot

to make sure his ankle wouldn't hurt.

"Much better," he said happily. "Now, let us beat those Sheldon Slammers!"

The Bailey Batters cheered and headed for the field. It wasn't long before they realized they were in trouble. Big trouble.

"It's only the third inning, and we're already behind by five runs," Eddie complained.

Melody nodded. "I can't believe I missed that fly ball. I never miss."

"And I never strike out," Howie groaned. "But I've struck out twice already."

"Luck just wasn't on our side," Liza said. "We'll do better."

The crack of the bat hitting the ball interrupted them, and the Bailey Batters watched a Sheldon Slammer's ball fly over the fence.

"So much for luck," Eddie complained. "It's time that new coach gave us some pointers!"

Eddie, Melody, Liza, and Howie jogged over to Coach Tuttle. "The Sheldon Slammers are beating the stripes off our uniforms! We need your help. Bad!" Melody told him.

"Yes, yes. Of course. Let me help you with your swing. Watch closely." Coach Tuttle grabbed a bat and hefted it to his shoulder. Then he took a huge swing. When he did, the bat flew from his hands, sailed over the bleachers, and crashed right through the window of the Sheldon Slammers' coach's car.

"Oops!" Coach Tuttle grabbed his right wrist and grinned at the kids. "Perhaps that is not the best way to swing a bat!"

"Are you okay?" Melody asked.

"Just a little sprained wrist. That is all," Coach Tuttle told her.

"That's going to be the least of your pain," Eddie warned, "because here comes Coach Snarley."

3

Walking Disaster

"I've never seen Coach Snarley so mad." Eddie laughed and pitched a softball to Howie. It was two days after the game and the Bailey Batters were practicing at Antwerp Field.

The ball bounced on the ground before Howie could catch it. A big spotted dog darted from the shadows of the bleachers and grabbed the ball.

"Diamond!" Eddie yelled. "Give that back!" The big dog just wagged his tail.

"Why did you bring your aunt's dog, anyway?" Melody complained. Every time the ball touched the ground, the playful dog tried to get it. Then the Bailey Batters had to chase him to get the ball back.

Eddie trotted over to Diamond and

grabbed the ball from his mouth. He wiped it on his pants before tossing the ball to Howie. "Aunt Mathilda couldn't take him on his walk today, so I told her I would do it," Eddie told Melody. "He's not hurting anything. Just don't drop the ball again!"

Howie caught the ball and threw it to Liza. Liza threw an underhanded pitch to Melody. Melody caught the ball and looked at Eddie. "You know," Melody said, "if it wasn't for Coach Tuttle we would have lost to the Sheldon Slammers."

Liza nodded. "Coach Tuttle was good luck for us."

"How can you say that?" Eddie said. "He didn't help us at all."

Howie disagreed. "Yes, he did. Coach Snarley was so upset about his car, he had to postpone the game. Now, we still have a chance to beat them."

Melody pitched the ball back to Eddie. "I have a feeling that Coach Tuttle is really special and that he's going to help us win the championship this year."

Eddie caught the ball and shook his head. "I'm afraid Coach Tuttle isn't much of a coach. He's a walking disaster." Eddie pointed to the parking lot. Coach Tuttle was getting bats and balls out of the trunk of his station wagon. Most of the balls and bats ended up dropping onto the ground, bouncing all around him. Every time he picked up a bat, he dropped two more.

Coach Tuttle reached out to pick up a ball and slipped on another ball. He came down hard on his left elbow. "Ye-ow!" he screamed.

"A walking disaster," Eddie repeated, shaking his head.

Before Eddie could stop him, Diamond raced across the field to Coach Tuttle.

The friendly dog grabbed one of the bats Coach Tuttle was holding and tried to play tug-of-war.

"Come on," Liza said. "We better help him." Liza, Melody, and Howie ran to the coach's car and picked up the bats and balls. Eddie grabbed Diamond by the collar and pulled hard until the dog let go of the bat.

"I'm sorry," Eddie told the coach. "Diamond just wants to play."

"Diamond?" Coach Tuttle said. "What a perfect name for such a valuable pet."

"Did you hurt yourself?" Howie asked Coach Tuttle.

"Just a little scratch," Coach Tuttle said. "I'll be fine in a minute."

The four kids watched as Coach Tuttle opened up his black leather bag and pulled out his big ball of white elastic bandage.

In just a few minutes, Coach Tuttle

wrapped his elbow in white. Diamond tried to grab the end of the bandage, but Coach Tuttle whipped it away and tucked in the end. Eddie grabbed Diamond's collar to pull him away, while the rest of the kids helped pick up the fallen bats and balls. Then they headed back to the playing field.

Eddie whispered to Liza on their way back to the field. "If Coach Tuttle keeps wrapping himself in those white bandages, he'll look like a sloppy spring snowman."

Liza giggled, but then she stopped laughing. "Either that, or a mummy," she whispered.

4

Ye-ow!

Eddie made Diamond go back to the bleachers and the Bailey Batters ran out onto the field and waited for Coach Tuttle to tell them their positions. Coach Tuttle walked slowly onto the field, carrying his black bag.

"All right!" Melody cheered. "Let's play ball."

"What's taking Coach Tuttle so long?" Eddie complained. "Practice will be over before he even gets here."

"He can't help it," Melody explained. "That bandage on his ankle makes it hard for him to walk."

Howie bent down to tie his cleats and looked at the huge bandage on Coach Tuttle's leg. "I know I'm not a doctor," he

19

said. "But it seems like an awfully big bandage for such a little accident."

"People in hospitals don't have that much gauze on them," Eddie agreed.

Liza dropped the balls and bats in her hands onto the ground and looked at Coach Tuttle. "I think he's just trying to be careful. Maybe the extra bandages make him feel better."

"He's going to need something to feel better," Eddie said.

The whole team looked just in time to see Coach Tuttle slip on one of the balls Liza had dropped. CRASH! Coach Tuttle plopped onto the ground. His black bag flew into the air and then came back down with a thud, right on top of his head. "Ye-ow!" he screamed.

Diamond barked loudly and the Bailey Batters rushed to Coach Tuttle. "I'm so sorry," Liza said. "It's all my fault!"

"Not to worry," Coach Tuttle said,

rubbing his head. "I will be fine in just a minute."

The whole team watched as Coach Tuttle wrapped his left knee and then the top of his head in the white bandages.

"This new coach is the pits," Eddie said to his friends. "He has more accidents than any man alive."

"That is *if* he's alive," Liza said softly.

"What?" Eddie, Melody, and Howie said together.

Liza pulled her friends away from Coach Tuttle and looked at them seriously. "I think Coach Tuttle is a mummy."

Eddie laughed. "Your baseball cap must be too tight. It's cutting off the blood to your brain. Coach Tuttle might be an accident waiting to happen, but he's no mummy."

"He sure *looks* like a mummy," Melody whispered, looking over at their new coach. He now had two legs, two arms, and his head wrapped in white bandages. The rest of the team gathered around him as he wrote their names on a clipboard. The papers on the clipboard kept falling off and Coach Tuttle spent most of his time on the ground picking them up.

Howie shook his head. "Coach Tuttle is clumsy all right, but he is a normal man."

"Yeah," Eddie agreed. "Mummies are dead guys wrapped in toilet paper. Coach Tuttle is definitely alive."

"Maybe you're right," Melody said. "After all, mummies don't coach softball."

Howie pulled on his softball glove. "Think about it, Liza. What would a mummy be doing in Bailey City?"

"I have thought about it," Liza told him. "And I think I know the answer."

"Well, don't keep us waiting in the pyramids," Howie said. "Tell us why a mummy would spend his vacation here."

"Maybe he wants to play gin rummy with a dummy," Eddie said.

Liza glared at Eddie, but he kept on teasing. "He probably heard that Dover's Department Store has free gift wrapping." Eddie giggled and poked Howie in the stomach. "Get it?" Eddie said. "Free wrapping."

Howie laughed. "Maybe he likes their white sale!"

Liza stomped her foot. "Stop kidding around. Don't you remember the Shelley Museum?"

Melody, Howie, and Eddie stopped laughing. They had gone to the Shelley Museum on a field trip. What they remembered most was being scared by the director's assistant, who looked like Frankenstein's monster.

"What about the museum?" Howie asked.

"It has an exhibit about Bill Antwerp," Liza explained.

24

"What does a twerp have to do with a mummy?" Eddie asked.

Liza rolled her eyes. "Bill Antwerp was one of the richest people who ever lived in Bailey City. He built this softball field."

"I still don't see what he has to do with Coach Tuttle," Melody said.

Liza lowered her voice and spoke slowly. "Bill Antwerp is the reason a mummy is in Bailey City!"

5

Mummy of Doom

"Let's get started," Coach Tuttle yelled before Liza could explain. "Eddie, you play first base. Melody, you can be short-stop and Howie can play third base." Kids ran all over the field as Coach Tuttle called out their positions. When everyone was in place, Coach Tuttle started hitting balls for them to catch. He had them catching grounders and pop flies all afternoon.

After practice, Liza pulled her friends to the shadows of the bleachers. "The Shelley Museum told the real story about Bill Antwerp. Many years ago, a stranger came to Bailey City," Liza began.

"That's nothing," Eddie interrupted.

"Bailey City is full of strange people. Like Liza!"

"Shh," Melody warned Eddie. "Let her finish."

"This stranger was said to have been the most unlucky person to ever have set foot in Bailey City," Liza said.

"Just living in Bailey City is unlucky if you ask me," Eddie joked.

Howie glared at Eddie. "What happened to the stranger?"

"First, he lost his prized Egyptian cat. Then, his house burned down. All he escaped with was his life and his mysterious diamond."

"Yeah, yeah, yeah," Eddie muttered. "So what does an unlucky twerp have to do with our clumsy new coach?"

"Antwerp," Liza snapped. "His name was Antwerp. The mysterious Antwerp was a wealthy man, and he loved diamonds. He wore diamonds on every finger. He even had diamond buttons on his coat and diamond buttons on his shirts. That's why he built Antwerp softball field."

"I don't get it," Melody interrupted. "What does Mr. Antwerp's love of shiny rocks have to do with a softball field?"

"Must I tell you everything?" Liza asked. "A baseball field has the biggest diamond of all." Liza pointed to the field and the bases that made up the baseball diamond. "But there was one very special

diamond. People called it the famous Antwerp Diamond."

"What's so famous about the Antwerp Diamond?" Howie asked.

"When the light of the rising sun hit it, the huge diamond glowed like a pyramid in the desert sun. Just like the fabled Egyptian stone buried with the Mummy of Doom."

"Mummy of Doom?" her three friends said together.

Liza nodded. "Whoever disturbed the sacred tomb where the fabled diamond was buried was cursed by the Mummy of Doom." Liza glanced around Antwerp Field. A few Bailey Batters were tossing a softball in the outfield, but nobody was close enough to hear. Liza whispered anyway. "Some people think Antwerp stole the cursed diamond right from the clutches of the Mummy of Doom himself."

Eddie giggled and even Howie smiled. Melody patted Liza on the arm. "That's a nice story," she told her friend, "but we don't understand what it has to do with Coach Tuttle."

Liza put her hands on her hips and stomped her foot so hard a dust cloud covered their cleats. "Laugh all you want," she snapped. "But you won't think it's so funny when you find out Coach Tuttle is the Mummy of Doom and he's here to get his diamond back!"

Eddie laughed so hard he fell back against the bleachers. "The only thing we're doomed with is listening to Liza's crazy ideas!"

"Besides that," Howie added, "Coach Tuttle can't find his way to home plate without help. Let alone find a diamond in all of Bailey City."

"We don't have time to worry about Liza's silly Mummy of Doom," Eddie told them. "We have to worry about beating Coach Snarley and his Sheldon Slammers."

"That's right," Howie agreed. "Our makeup game is two days away."

Liza shook her head. "There's no use worrying. No team has ever won a home game at Antwerp Field. Antwerp Field has been a curse to the Bailey Batters ever since it was built. Cursed by the Mummy of Doom."

"But why would a mummy care about cursing the Antwerp softball diamond?" Melody asked.

"Not unless," Liza said slowly, "Coach Tuttle is confused."

"Coach Tuttle is very confused," Eddie said. "Just like you are. Now stop talking this mummy madness. We need to figure out how to beat the Sheldon Slammers."

The four friends looked over at Antwerp Field. Huey and Carey were pitching the ball. Carey missed an easy throw and the ball whopped her right on the shoulder.

"*Ouch!*" Carey screamed.

Coach Tuttle ran from the parking lot with his little black bag. In a few minutes, Carey's shoulder was wrapped in white bandages.

"Liza's right about one thing," Eddie said. "Our team is doomed."

"Unless we do something quick," Howie said, "those Sheldon Slammers are going to grind us into diamond dust."

Liza nodded. "And Coach Tuttle is going to turn us all into mummies!"

6

Lucky Ducky

The next afternoon Liza, Melody, Howie, and Eddie were early for practice. "Come on," Eddie said as they walked onto the softball field. "We have to practice hard to get ready for the Sheldon Slammers."

"Coach Tuttle is already here," Howie told them. "Maybe he can give us some pointers." The four friends looked at Coach Tuttle. He was down on his knees using his hands to throw dirt away from third base.

"He looks as if he's digging for something," Melody said.

Eddie snickered. "Maybe he's looking for a better coach."

Howie walked toward their coach.

"He's just getting the field ready for us," he explained.

Coach Tuttle jumped up when he saw the four kids and started kicking dirt back around third base. His hands were red from digging, so he wrapped more bandages around them. "Welcome, boys and girls," he called. "Are you ready to practice?"

Coach Tuttle had the team pitching, catching, running bases, and hitting. They didn't stop working for ninety minutes. By then, Liza was panting and Howie's face was red.

"Good work, boys and girls," Coach Tuttle called. "With hard work like this, you will do well against the Slammers."

"All right!" the team cheered.

Melody smiled as Coach Tuttle walked off the field. "Our coach may look like a reject from the pyramids, but maybe he knows what he's doing after all. That was a great practice."

Eddie sat down on the ground and took off his cleats. "It didn't have anything to do with Coach Tuttle," he told his friends. "I'm the one who made practice great."

Liza folded her arms in front of her. "And exactly how did you do that?"

Eddie stuck his foot up in the air. He was wearing white socks with bright yellow ducks on them. "My lucky ducky socks made it happen. Not only that, I spit in my hat and I'm wearing my lucky underwear. I'm super lucky!"

"Maybe not lucky enough," Melody said, pointing toward the parking lot. Coach Tuttle closed the back door to his station wagon. On the way down, the door hit him right in the neck.

"Ye-ow!" Coach Tuttle screamed. Then he unrolled a long white bandage from his black bag and wrapped it around his neck. Now his head, neck, arms, hands,

and both legs were wrapped in big white bandages.

"Coach Tuttle needs some luck," Howie said. "He looks like a big ball of spaghetti."

"No," Liza said softly. "Coach Tuttle needs the Antwerp Diamond. And we're going to help him find it!"

7

The Clancy Estate

"Follow me," Liza called as she ran toward Forest Lane. Her three friends shrugged, then took off after her. They looked both ways, crossed Forest Lane, and then cut across the soccer field. They stopped in front of the old Clancy estate on Delaware Boulevard.

"What are we doing here?" Eddie asked. "This place gives me the creeps."

Most people in Bailey City considered the Clancy estate haunted. The four kids figured their third grade teacher, Mrs. Jeepers, was a vampire when she moved into the big Victorian house.

"This place was built by Bill Antwerp," Liza explained. "It's one of the oldest houses in Bailey City."

Howie looked up at the pointy roof of

the old house. "I thought old man Clancy built it."

Liza shook her head. "According to the museum exhibit, Mr. Clancy bought it after Bill Antwerp died."

Melody stared at Liza. "I thought you said the Antwerp mansion burned to the ground."

"It did," Liza agreed. "This was just the gatehouse for the huge Antwerp mansion. Mr. Antwerp lived here after the mansion burned."

"Where was the mansion?" Howie asked.

Liza pointed across the soccer field to Bailey Elementary School.

"You mean our school is built on the ashes of the Antwerp mansion?" Melody asked.

Liza nodded. "The cursed Antwerp mansion," she said softly.

"I always thought Bailey Elementary

was cursed." Eddie laughed. "Now I know why."

"But I still don't know why we're here," Howie said.

"Don't you get it?" Liza asked. "The Antwerp Diamond must still be hidden somewhere inside this old house. If we find it, we'll return it to Coach Tuttle, and the curse will be removed."

"There's just one small problem," Melody reminded her. "Mrs. Jeepers lives here now."

Howie and Eddie looked at each other and gulped. Their teacher was definitely strange.

"Don't knock on her door!" Howie said. "She might suck our blood!"

But it was too late. Liza had already let the huge door knocker fall against the heavy wooden door.

"Now you've done it," Eddie moaned. "We're bound to be bat bait!"

"It's not too late," Melody said. "We can run away before Mrs. Jeepers gets to the door."

Just then, the heavy wooden door slowly creaked open. Melody, Howie, and Eddie took a huge step back, but Liza just smiled up at their third grade teacher.

Mrs. Jeepers stood in the shadows and peered down at the four students standing on her porch. She wore a black dress that touched the top of her pointy-toed boots, and her long red hair was pulled back in a ponytail. Pinned to her collar was the mysterious green brooch she always wore. "Good afternoon," she said in her strange Transylvanian accent. "What a pleasant surprise."

"We hate to bother you," Liza said in her most polite voice. "But we're doing some research and we need your help."

Melody stepped up behind Liza. "We really liked the research we did last

month, so we decided to do some of our own," she lied.

"About Bailey City," Howie added.

Liza nodded. "We're trying to find out about the famous Bill Antwerp, the man who built the softball field."

"We know he built your house," Melody said. "We were wondering if we could look around."

"Maybe he left some things here that we could see," Liza added.

Mrs. Jeepers smiled an odd little half smile. "I checked the entire house when I moved in," she told them. "Except . . . "

"Except for what?" Liza asked.

"I have not been through the attic," she told her students. "All of my belongings are stored in the basement."

Eddie's eyes got big and Melody shivered even though the sun was shining brightly. They both remembered the night they sneaked into their teacher's basement and found a long wooden box.

They were sure that's where Mrs. Jeepers' vampire husband slept.

"Perhaps you will find something in the attic. Follow me," Mrs. Jeepers said and disappeared into the dim light of the Clancy estate.

Eddie grabbed Liza's elbow. "We can't go in there," he whispered. "She probably keeps vampire bats in her attic."

"The only bats around here are on the softball field," Liza said. Then she pulled her arm away and disappeared inside.

8

Far from Home

"We can't let her go alone," Melody said softly.

"Yes, we can," Eddie argued.

"Melody's right," Howie told Eddie. "If Liza's brave enough, then I am too. Let's go!"

Howie pushed Eddie inside. Melody followed them and shut the door with a loud click. The three friends looked up at the cobwebs draped on the huge chandelier hanging above their heads.

"Mrs. Jeepers may be a good teacher, but she's a terrible housekeeper," Howie whispered.

"This way," Liza called to her friends. Liza stood at the top of the massive wooden staircase that curved down from the second floor.

Melody took a deep breath and slowly climbed the steps covered in blood-red carpet. Eddie and Howie followed close behind.

"This is the door to the attic," Liza told her friends.

"Where's Mrs. Jeepers?" Howie asked, his voice a whisper.

Liza pointed down the hall to a closed door. "She's reading a huge book. She told me we could look around all we want."

Liza led her friends up the creaky steps to the attic. Cobwebs brushed against their faces and their sneakers stirred up a thick cloud of dust. The attic was completely empty except for an old crate in the far corner.

"Ah-choo!" Melody sneezed. "There's nothing up here but dust bunnies."

"I bet that was Mr. Antwerp's!" Liza said, before rushing to push the lid off the crate.

The four friends stared at piles of pictures of a land filled with desert sand and tall pyramids.

"Whoever owned this box must have liked to travel," Eddie said.

"Maybe," Liza said softly. "Or maybe he was homesick."

"What are you talking about?" Eddie asked.

Liza shrugged. "I think Mr. Antwerp kept these pictures because he wanted to go home."

"Then why didn't he just go?" Howie asked.

"Because," Liza told her friends. "He stole the cursed diamond from the Mummy of Doom. It wasn't safe to go home again."

Melody sighed. "It would be terrible to be so far from home."

"It will be terrible if you don't stop talking about this mummy stuff," Eddie said. "We don't have time to waste snooping around this dusty attic and talking about a mummy's home. The only home we need to worry about is home plate, because the game against the Sheldon Slammers is tomorrow!"

Just then, Liza looked at Eddie and shrieked.

Eddie yelled and Melody jumped back. When Melody jumped, she fell into Howie and he tripped over the crate. They both landed on the floor.

Liza looked at her friends and giggled. "There's no need to be so jumpy."

"Then why did you yell?" Howie sputtered.

"Because Eddie just figured out the answer to the mystery," Liza said.

"What mystery?" Eddie asked.

Liza rolled her eyes. "Where Bill Antwerp hid the missing Antwerp Diamond, silly. All we have to do is get the diamond and break the curse. Then we'll win against the Sheldon Slammers."

Eddie stood up tall and grinned. "I knew I could do it."

Howie wasn't impressed. He got up, brushing the dust off the seat of his jeans. "So where is this famous diamond?" he asked Eddie. "There's nothing in this box but old photographs."

Eddie shifted from one foot to the other. "Well ... it's ... you see ..." Eddie sputtered. Then he looked at Liza. "Yeah, where is it?"

"It's simple!" Liza told her friends. "It's right where Mr. Antwerp wanted to be. Home."

"But he was home," Howie pointed out. "Right here in Bailey City."

Liza shook her head. "Egypt was his real home."

"Then we are doomed," Melody said. "We can't go to Egypt to find the diamond."

"We won't have to," Liza grinned.

"You're not making any sense," Howie

argued. "First you say it's at Antwerp's Egyptian home, then you say it isn't. Make up your mind."

Liza skipped across the dusty floor to the attic door. "Wait until the sun goes down and meet me at Antwerp Field," she told her friends. "Then it will all make sense." And then Liza disappeared down the attic steps of the Clancy estate.

9

There's No Place Like Home

The sun was just sinking behind distant Ruby Mountain when Howie, Melody, and Eddie cut across the soccer field and jogged down Forest Lane toward Antwerp Field.

Eddie held a leash so his Great-aunt Mathilda's giant spotted dog wouldn't get away.

"Why did you bring Diamond?" Melody asked.

"I told my grandma I would walk him," Eddie said. "It's the only way she'd let me out of the house. Besides, I figured since his name is Diamond, he'd bring us good luck."

"Oh, Eddie," Melody said. "There's no such thing as luck."

"My good luck charms have worked so far," Eddie argued. "Now let's get this mummy stuff all wrapped up so we can figure out how we can win the championship game tomorrow."

They hadn't gone far when they spotted Liza. The three friends hollered and Liza slowed down to wait for them. A red sand bucket and shovel dangled from her left hand.

"What's that for?" Melody pointed to the shovel and bucket that Diamond was busy sniffing.

"Are you planning on building sand castles?" Eddie giggled.

Liza held up the plastic shovel. "Maybe I need this to shovel some sense into your head."

Howie held up his hand. "Calm down, Liza. You have to admit carrying a sand bucket and shovel in the middle of town is a little strange."

"The only thing strange around Bailey

City is Coach Tuttle," Liza told him. "But if Eddie is right, we won't have to worry about him much longer."

"If I'm right about what?" Eddie asked.

"Mr. Antwerp saved that box of pictures because he wanted to go home," Liza explained.

"But you said he couldn't," Melody reminded her.

"Exactly," Liza said. "So he did the next best thing. He built the Antwerp softball diamond, complete with a home of its own."

"*Home plate!*" Eddie yelled so loud that Diamond barked.

"Where he hid the cursed diamond," Liza finished.

"That would explain why no Bailey team has ever won a home game," Melody said.

"Until tomorrow," Liza said with a grin.

Liza led her friends the rest of the way to Antwerp Field. But in the gray light of dusk, the four friends saw a dark figure huddled over home plate. Eddie pulled Diamond into the deep shadows of the bleachers and Howie, Melody, and Liza scooted in after them.

"Who could that be?" Melody whispered.

"Shh," Howie warned and pointed.

The figure stood up and peered into the shadows of the bleachers. Melody, Liza, Howie, and Eddie held their breaths and watched the bulky person take one step, then another toward their hiding place. Step by step, closer and closer he came.

Melody whimpered and Liza closed her eyes. Howie got ready to scream and Eddie was so scared he squeezed Diamond.

The dog growled deep in his throat and stared at the stranger. Before Eddie could stop him, Diamond raced across the field toward the shadowy figure.

"*Stop!*" Eddie screamed. But Diamond

didn't listen. Diamond chased the stranger off the field and clear across the parking lot. He didn't stop until the stranger disappeared down the street. Then Diamond trotted back across the field and licked Eddie's hand.

"Who do you think that was?" Melody asked.

Liza pointed. "That should tell you the answer."

There, scattered all over Antwerp's softball field, were tiny piles of dirt.

"You don't honestly believe that Coach Tuttle spent the afternoon building sand castles, do you?" Eddie asked.

"If Liza's right," Howie said, "Coach Tuttle is searching for the mummy's diamond."

"Then if that was your silly Mummy of Doom," Eddie said, "our problem is over."

"Not quite," Melody said. She led her friends to home plate. "There's no pyramid here, and if Liza's right, this is where the mummy's stolen treasure is hidden."

"We have to dig it up!" Liza dropped to the ground and tossed home plate aside. "And we have to hurry!"

10

Holy Moley

"Holy Moley!" Eddie screamed when a huge suntanned hand grabbed his shoulder. He looked up into Coach Ellison's angry face.

"What are you kids doing?" Coach Ellison bellowed. "You've ruined the softball field. It has more holes than a golf course!"

"But we didn't ... " Eddie tried to explain.

Coach Ellison shook his head. "I've

never seen such a mess. I have half a mind to take another cruise."

"Please don't," Liza said. "We need you to help us beat the Sheldon Slammers tomorrow."

"That's why I asked Coach Tuttle to help," Coach Ellison told them. "I didn't know you were going to make Swiss cheese out of the field."

"But it was Coach Tuttle who ... " Melody started to tell him.

"Never mind," Coach Ellison snapped. "The game is at one o'clock tomorrow. That means you can spend all morning filling in the holes before the game."

"What?" Eddie shrieked. Scooping dirt on a softball field was not how he wanted to spend his Saturday morning.

"That's right," Coach Ellison said, crossing his arms over his chest. "I want every hole filled in tight. We don't want anyone tripping and falling halfway to China. Now, take that mutt and get home before I really get mad!" Coach Ellison stomped off before Eddie could complain again.

"Yes, sir," Liza, Melody, and Howie said together. Diamond was still digging at home plate, and Eddie had to drag him away. They were halfway across the field when the dog jerked away from Eddie and ran back to home plate.

Diamond was digging like a crazy bulldozer when Eddie grabbed his collar. "Stop it," Eddie yelled. "We have enough holes to fill in tomorrow without you making this one deeper." Diamond whined, but Eddie pulled him hard.

"I can't believe we have to fill in all those holes," Melody complained as they walked down the sidewalk on Forest Lane.

"I can't believe we didn't find the cursed diamond. If someone doesn't find it," Liza warned, "we all may be doomed."

11

Treasure

"Liza, this is all your fault," Eddie snapped as he filled in the last bit of dirt near home plate and stomped it in tight with his foot. "This hole was even bigger than it was last night." It was Saturday morning and the kids had been working for over an hour to fill in the holes.

Liza giggled and sat on the ground. "Holes don't just dig themselves," she said.

"Maybe Diamond came back and dug some more," Howie suggested. "He looks awfully tired this morning." Diamond was lying beside third base. He was sound asleep and snoring.

"He can't be any more tired than me," Melody said. "My arms are worn out from all this work."

"But you did a great job," Coach Ellison said as he stepped onto the field. "Everything is back to normal."

"Even Coach Tuttle," Liza gasped, and pointed. Coach Ellison and the four kids looked at the parking lot. Coach Tuttle was pulling bats and balls from his station wagon. His bandages were all gone and he didn't drop a single ball or bat. He even managed to close the station wagon door without hitting his head.

"He's like a totally different person," Melody said.

Howie shook his head as Coach Ellison went to talk to Coach Tuttle. Coach Tuttle shook hands with Coach Ellison without dropping a ball or bat. "I don't get it," Howie said. "How can he be so different?"

"I understand," Liza told them. "The curse of the Mummy of Doom has been lifted. Coach Tuttle must have found the treasure."

"There's only one curse around here," Eddie said, pointing to a group of Sheldon Slammers coming onto the field.

"We don't have time to worry about the curse," Melody said. "We have to make our own good luck."

"Melody's right," Eddie said. Then he spit in his baseball cap and slapped it back on his head. "Besides, I wore my lucky socks and underwear! There's no way those Sheldon Slammers can beat us now!"

When Howie, Liza, Melody, and Eddie jogged over to Coach Ellison and Coach Tuttle, Diamond woke up and ran with them. He yelped the minute he saw Coach Tuttle. Then the big dog jumped up and licked Coach Tuttle right on his face.

"Diamond," Eddie commanded. "Get down!"

"That is all right, Eddie. Diamond is a treasure." Coach Tuttle laughed. "A real treasure!"

Debbie Dadey and Marcia Thornton Jones have fun writing stories together. When they both worked at an elementary school in Lexington, Kentucky, Debbie was the school librarian and Marcia was a teacher. During their lunch break in the school cafeteria, they came up with the idea of the Bailey School kids.

Recently Debbie and her family moved to Aurora, Illinois. Marcia and her husband still live in Kentucky where she continues to teach. How do these authors still write together? They talk on the phone and use computers and fax machines!

The Adventures of THE BAILEY SCHOOL KIDS™

Mrs. Jeepers invites the whole class to a party at her house. Then she disappears! Did Mrs. Jeepers *really* turn into a vampire at her own party?

This extra special, extra spooky Bailey School Kids adventure includes lots of monster-ously fun activities and puzzlcs. Plus, it comes with a poster of all your favorite Bailey School characters and 10 glow-in-the-dark fingers—just like Mrs. Jeepers!

The Adventures of The Bailey School Kids Super Special #1

Mrs. Jeepers Is Missing

by Debbie Dadey and Marcia Thornton Jones.

Coming to a bookstore near you.

Creepy, weird, wacky and funny things happen to the Bailey School Kids!™ Collect and read them all!

☐ BAS43411-X	#1	Vampires Don't Wear Polka Dots	$2.99
☐ BAS44061-6	#2	Werewolves Don't Go to Summer Camp	$2.99
☐ BAS44477-8	#3	Santa Claus Doesn't Mop Floors	$2.99
☐ BAS44822-6	#4	Leprechauns Don't Play Basketball	$2.99
☐ BAS45854-X	#5	Ghosts Don't Eat Potato Chips	$2.99
☐ BAS47071-X	#6	Frankenstein Doesn't Plant Petunias	$2.99
☐ BAS47070-1	#7	Aliens Don't Wear Braces	$2.99
☐ BAS47297-6	#8	Genies Don't Ride Bicycles	$2.99
☐ BAS47298-4	#9	Pirates Don't Wear Pink Sunglasses	$2.99
☐ BAS48112-6	#10	Witches Don't Do Backflips	$2.99
☐ BAS48113-4	#11	Skeletons Don't Play Tubas	$2.99
☐ BAS48114-2	#12	Cupid Doesn't Flip Hamburgers	$2.99
☐ BAS48115-0	#13	Gremlins Don't Chew Bubble Gum	$2.99
☐ BAS22635-5	#14	Monsters Don't Scuba Dive	$2.99
☐ BAS22636-3	#15	Zombies Don't Play Soccer	$2.99
☐ BAS22638-X	#16	Dracula Doesn't Drink Lemonade	$2.99
☐ BAS22637-1	#17	Elves Don't Wear Hard Hats	$2.99
☐ BAS50960-8	#18	Martians Don't Take Temperatures	$2.99
☐ BAS50961-6	#19	Gargoyles Don't Drive School Buses	$2.99
☐ BAS50962-4	#20	Wizards Don't Need Computers	$2.99
☐ BAS22639-8	#21	Mummies Don't Coach Softball	$2.99
☐ BAS84886-0	#22	Cyclops Doesn't Roller-Skate	$2.99
☐ BAS84902-6	#23	Angels Don't Know Karate	$2.99
☐ BAS84904-2	#24	Dragons Don't Cook Pizza	$2.99
☐ BAS84905-0	#25	Bigfoot Doesn't Square Dance	$3.50
☐ BAS84906-9	#26	Mermaids Don't Run Track	$3.50
☐ BAS25701-3	#27	Bogeymen Don't Play Football	$3.50
☐ BAS99552-9		Bailey School Kids Joke Book	$3.50
☐ BAS88134-5		Bailey School Kids Super Special #1: Mrs. Jeepers Is Missing!	$4.99
☐ BAS21243-5		Bailey School Kids Super Special #2: Mrs. Jeepers' Batty Vacation	$4.99

Available wherever you buy books, or use this order form

Scholastic Inc., P.O. Box 7502, Jefferson City, MO 65102

Please send me the books I have checked above. I am enclosing $_____ (please add $2.00 to cover shipping and handling). Send check or money order — no cash or C.O.D.s please.

Name _____

Address _____

City_____ State/Zip _____

Please allow four to six weeks for delivery. Offer good in the U.S. only. Sorry, mail orders are not available to residents of Canada. Prices subject to change.   BSK397